FURTHER DOINGS OF
MILLY-MOLLY-MANDY

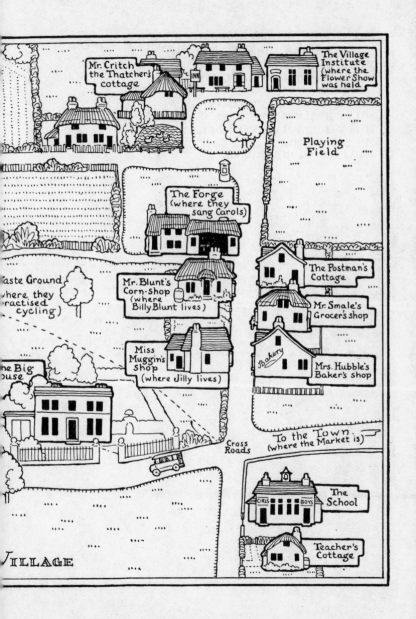

Mr. Critch the Thatcher's cottage

INN

The Village Institute (where the Flower Show was held)

Playing Field

The Forge (where they sang Carols)

The Postman's Cottage

Mr. Blunt's Corn-shop (where Billy Blunt lives)

Mr. Smale's Grocer's shop

Waste Ground (where they practised cycling)

Miss Muggin's shop (where Jilly lives)

Bakery

Mrs. Hubble's Baker's shop

The Big House

To the Town (where the Market is)

Cross Roads

GIRLS BOYS

The School

Teacher's Cottage

VILLAGE

FURTHER DOINGS OF
MILLY-MOLLY-MANDY

TOLD AND DRAWN
BY
JOYCE LANKESTER BRISLEY

GEORGE G. HARRAP & COMPANY LTD
LONDON TORONTO WELLINGTON SYDNEY

*I wish to make grateful acknowledgment
to "The Christian Science Monitor" for
permission to reprint these stories, which,
with the larger drawings, first appeared
in the Children's Page of that paper.*

J. L. B.

First published in Great Britain May 1932
by George G. Harrap & Co. Ltd
182-184 High Holborn, London WC1V 7AX

Reprinted: 1933; 1934 (*twice*); 1935; 1936; 1937; 1938
(*twice*); 1939 (*twice*); 1940; 1941 (*twice*); 1942 (*twice*);
1943; 1944; 1945; 1946; 1948; 1949; 1951; 1953 (*twice*);
1955; 1956; 1959; 1961; 1963; 1964; 1966; 1968; 1971

ISBN 0 245 56155 2

*Reproduced and Printed in Great Britain by
Redwood Press Limited
Trowbridge & London*

CONTENTS

FURTHER DOINGS OF
MILLY-MOLLY-MANDY

I

Milly-Molly-Mandy Has a Tea-party

ONCE upon a time Milly-Molly-Mandy had a nice little surprise.

Uncle came back from market one Saturday with a square cardboard box under the seat of the pony-trap, and he gave it to Milly-Molly-Mandy to hold while he got his other parcels out. It was a neat little whity-brown box, tied round with string, and it wasn't very heavy, and it didn't rattle much, and it didn't smell of anything except cardboard, and Milly-Molly-Mandy couldn't guess what was in it. So she asked Uncle.

And Uncle said, " Oh, just some odd bits of things I want to get rid of. Throw them away for me, Milly-Molly-Mandy ! "

Milly-Molly-Mandy looked at Uncle in surprise, for it didn't seem the sort of box to be thrown away. She thought Uncle was looking a bit twinkly, so she said, " I'd better just peep in it first before I throw it away, hadn't I, Uncle ? "

And Uncle, gathering up his parcels, said, " Oh, yes, yes. We don't want to make any mistake about

9

Milly-Molly-Mandy

it," and went off with them toward the kitchen door.

So Milly-Molly-Mandy picked the knot undone, and when she got the box open what DO you think she saw inside? The sweetest little dolls' tea-set, with cups and plates and milk-jug and all complete, fitted neatly in holes cut in the cardboard so that they shouldn't rattle about!

Milly-Molly-Mandy gave a squeak of excitement and put the box down on the ground in a hurry, while she ran after Uncle, crying, " Oh, Uncle, thank you! Is it for me? Oh, thank you, Uncle!" And Uncle pretended to be surprised, and said, "What's that? Wasn't it rubbish after all? Well, well, what a good thing you looked!" and went indoors with his parcels; and Milly-Molly-Mandy ran back to her tea-set.

It was the prettiest little tea-set, with a teapot that would really pour, and a sugar-basin with a tiny lid, and two little cups and saucers and plates—"One for me, and one for Susan," thought Milly-Molly-Mandy to herself. "I'll ask Mother if I can ask Susan to tea to-day."

So she carried the box into the kitchen (where Mother was busy taking the cakes out of the oven), and asked. And Mother admired the tea-set, and said, "Certainly, Milly-Molly-Mandy. And you may have this little cake on a saucer, and one of these little bread rolls to look like a loaf."

Has a Tea-party

So that afternoon Milly-Molly-Mandy laid a small cloth on the garden table and arranged her tea-set on it, with a little vase of flowers in the centre, and all the good things Mother had given her to eat ; and when everything was ready she ran down the white road with the hedges each side to ask little-friend-Susan to come to the tea-party.

But what do you think ?

Before she got as far as the Moggs's cottage (where little-friend-Susan lived) she met little-friend-Susan herself coming up to the nice white cottage with the thatched roof (where Milly-Molly-Mandy lived). And Milly-Molly-Mandy said, "Hullo, Susan! I was just coming to ask you to a dolls' tea-party. I've got a new tea-set !" And little-friend-Susan said just at the same moment, "Hullo, Milly-Molly-Mandy! I've got a new tea-set— will you come to a dolls' tea-party with me ? "

So then they both stopped still and stared at each other.

"Mine's a perfectly new tea-set," said Milly-Molly-Mandy. "Uncle brought it to me from market, and it's pink."

"I only had mine to-day," said little-friend-Susan. "Father brought it home from market, and it's blue."

"But I've got a special little cake and a proper loaf," said Milly-Molly-Mandy. "Do come ! "

"No, you come ! " said little-friend-Susan. "I've

Milly-Molly-Mandy

got a tiny little tart and a weeny little pot of strawberry jam!"

"I've got lots of bread-and-jam on an ordinary plate for us to eat," said Milly-Molly-Mandy, "and it is such a sweet little tea-set!"

"Oh, Milly-Molly-Mandy," said little-friend-Susan,

"mine's all laid in the summer-house, and there's a daisy beside each plate, and lots and lots of bread-and-dripping, and my tea-set is simply beautiful too!"

It was very difficult indeed to know what to do, for Milly-Molly-Mandy felt secretly sure that her party would be nicer, and she didn't want it wasted; and little-friend-Susan felt secretly sure too that her party would be nicer, and she didn't want it wasted either!

"Do come!" said Milly-Molly-Mandy.

"No, you come!" said little-friend-Susan.

Just then they saw Billy Blunt wandering down the road, scraping a bit of stick with his knife.

Milly-Molly-Mandy and little-friend-Susan were standing looking so solemn that Billy Blunt stopped and said, "What's up?"

So Milly-Molly-Mandy told him, and little-friend-Susan told him too. And Billy Blunt scraped away for a moment, and then said, "Better take your things into

12

Billy Blunt stopped and said, " What's up ?"

the meadow or somewhere and have a double tea."
(And he had his mouth open to add "And ask me

too," but he thought he'd
better not, in case they
didn't want him, so he
shut it again.)

And directly Milly-
Molly-Mandy and little-
friend-Susan heard that they both wondered why they
hadn't thought of a double tea themselves! Milly-
Molly-Mandy hopped on one leg, because she was so
pleased. And she said, "Then we shall each have a
cup over, so, Billy, you must come and have tea
too!"

So Milly-Molly-Mandy carried her little pink tea-set
out into the meadow; and little-friend-Susan carried
her little blue tea-set out into the meadow too; and
they all sat round on the grass and ate off the tiny

plates and drank out of the tiny
cups. And Milly-Molly-Mandy
poured out for little-friend-
Susan, and little-friend-Susan
poured out for Milly-Molly-
Mandy, and they both poured
out for Billy Blunt (who had two
cups all to himself, because he
was guest at two tea-parties)!

When they had finished eating (which happened when
there wasn't anything more to eat) they took the tea-
things to the brook at the bottom of the meadow and
washed them, and stood them on some moss to drain.

Minds a Baby

And Milly-Molly-Mandy and little-friend-Susan both thought a double tea-party was much more fun than just an ordinary one. And Billy Blunt (as the cups and plates were very small!) thought being a double guest was ever so much better than being just an ordinary single one!

So THAT was all right!

II

Milly-Molly-Mandy Minds a Baby

ONCE upon a time Milly-Molly-Mandy had to mind a tiny little baby.

It was the funniest, tiny little baby you could possibly imagine, and Milly-Molly-Mandy had to mind it because there didn't seem to be anybody else to do so. She couldn't find its mother or its father or any of its relations, so she had to take it home and look after it herself (because, of course, you can't leave a tiny little baby alone in a wood, with no one anywhere about to look after it).

And this is how it happened.

Milly-Molly-Mandy wanted some acorn-cups (which are useful for making dolls' bowls, and wheels for matchbox carts, and all that sort of thing, you know). So, as little-friend-Susan was busy looking after her baby sister, Milly-Molly-Mandy went off to the woods with just Toby the dog to look for some.

While she was busy looking she heard a loud chirping

noise. And Milly-Molly-Mandy said to herself, " I wonder what sort of bird that is ? " And then she found a ripe blackberry, and forgot about the chirping noise.

After a time Milly-Molly-Mandy said to herself, " How that bird does keep on chirping ! " And then Toby the dog found a rabbit-hole, and Milly-Molly-Mandy forgot again about the chirping noise.

After some more time Milly-Molly-Mandy said to herself, " That bird sounds as if it wants something." And then Milly-Molly-Mandy went toward a brambly clearing in the wood from which the chirping noise seemed to come.

But when she got there the chirping noise didn't seem to come from a tree, but from a low bramble-bush. And when she got to the low bramble-bush the chirping noise stopped.

Milly-Molly-Mandy thought that was because it was frightened of her. So she said out loud, " It's all right —don't be frightened. It's only me ! " just as kindly as she could, and then she poked about in among the bramble-bush. But she couldn't find anything, except thorns.

And then, quite suddenly, lying in the grass on the other side of the bramble-bush, Milly-Molly-Mandy and Toby the dog together found what had been making all the chirping noise. It was so frightened that it had rolled itself into a tight little prickly ball, no bigger than the penny indiarubber ball which Milly-Molly-Mandy had bought at Miss Muggins's shop the day before.

For what DO you think it was? A little tiny weeny baby hedgehog!

Milly-Molly-Mandy *was* excited! And so was Toby the dog! Milly-Molly-Mandy had to say, "No, Toby! Be quiet, Toby!" very firmly indeed. And then she picked up the baby hedgehog in a bracken leaf (because it was a  very prickly baby, though it was so small), and she could just see its little soft nose quivering among its prickles.

Then Milly-Molly-Mandy looked about to find its nest (for, of course, she didn't want to take it away from its family), but she couldn't find it. And then the baby began squeaking again for its mother, but its mother didn't come.

So at last Milly-Molly-Mandy said comfortingly, "Never mind, darling—I'll take you home and look after you!"

So Milly-Molly-Mandy carried the baby hedgehog between her two hands very carefully; and it unrolled itself a bit and quivered its little soft nose over her fingers as if it hoped they might be good to eat, and it

17

squeaked and squeaked, because it was very hungry. So Milly-Molly-Mandy hurried all she could, and Toby the dog capered along at her side, and at last they got home to the nice white cottage with the thatched roof.

Father and Mother and Grandpa and Grandma and Uncle and Aunty were all very interested indeed.

Mother put a saucer of milk on the stove to warm, and then they tried to feed the baby. But it was too little to lap from a saucer, and it was too little even to lick from Milly-Molly-Mandy's finger. So at last they had to wait until it opened its mouth to squeak and then squirt drops of warm milk into it with Father's fountain-pen filler!

After that the baby felt a bit happier, and Milly-Molly-Mandy made it a nest in a little box of hay. But when she put it in it squeaked and squeaked again for its nice warm mother till Milly-Molly-Mandy put her hand in the box; and then it snuggled up against it and went to sleep. And Milly-Molly-Mandy stood there and chuckled softly to herself, because it felt so funny being mistaken for Mrs Hedgehog! (She quite liked it!)

When Father and Grandpa and Uncle came in to dinner the baby woke and began squeaking again. So Uncle picked it up in his big hand to have a look at it, while Milly-Molly-Mandy ran for more milk and the fountain-pen filler.

And the baby squeaked so loudly that Uncle said, "Hul-lo, Horace! What's all this noise about?" And Milly-Molly-Mandy was pleased, because 'Horace' just seemed to suit the baby hedgehog, and no one

They were all very interested indeed

knew what its mother had named it (but I don't suppose it was Horace !).

Milly-Molly-Mandy was kept very busy all that day feeding Horace every hour or two. He was so prickly that she had to wrap him round in an old handkerchief

first—and he looked the funniest little baby in a white shawl you ever did see !

When bedtime came Milly-Molly-Mandy wanted to take the hedge-hog's box up to her little room with her. But Mother said no, he would be all right in the kitchen

till morning. So they gave him a hot bottle to snuggle against (it was an ink-bottle wrapped in flannel), and then Milly-Molly-Mandy went off to bed.

But being ' mother ' even to a hedgehog is a very important sort of job, and in the night Milly-Molly-Mandy woke up and thought of Horace, and wondered if he felt lonely in his new home.

And she creepy-crept in the dark to the top of the stairs and listened.

And after a time she heard a tiny little " Squeak ! squeak ! " coming from the kitchen. So she hurried and pulled on her dressing-gown and her bedroom slippers, and then she hurried and creepy-crept in the dark downstairs into the kitchen, and carefully lit the candle on the dresser.

And then she fed Horace and talked to him in a comfortable whisper, so that he didn't feel lonely any more. And then she put him back to bed and blew out the candle, and creepy-crept in the dark upstairs to her own little bed. (And it did feel so nice and warm to get into again!)

Next day Horace learned to open his mouth when he felt the fountain-pen filler touch it (he couldn't see, because his eyes weren't open yet—just like a baby puppy or kitten). And quite soon he learned to suck away at the filler just as if it were a proper baby's bottle! And he grew and he grew, and in a week's time his eyes were open. And soon he grew little

teeth, and could gobble bread and milk out of an egg-cup, and sometimes a little bit of meat or banana.

He was quite a little-boy hedgehog now, instead of a little baby one, and Milly-Molly-Mandy didn't need to get up in the night any more to feed him.

Milly-Molly-Mandy was very proud of him, and when little-friend-Susan used to say she had to hurry home after school to look after her baby sister, Milly-Molly-Mandy used to say she had to hurry too to look after the baby Horace. She used to give him walks in the garden, and laugh at his funny little back legs and tiny tail as he waddled about, nosing the ground. When Toby the dog barked he would roll himself up into a prickly ball in a second; but he soon came out again, and would run to Milly-Molly-Mandy's hand when she called "Horace!" (He was quite happy with her for a mother.)

Milly-Molly-Mandy

One day Horace got out of his hay-box in the kitchen, and they couldn't find him for a long time, though they all looked—Father and Mother and Grandpa and Grandma and Uncle and Aunty and Milly-Molly-Mandy. But at last where do you think they found him ?—in the larder !

" Well ! " said Uncle, " Horace knows how to look after himself all right now ! "

After that Horace's bed was put out in the barn, and Milly-Molly-Mandy would take his little basin of bread and milk out to him, and stay and play till it got too chilly.

And then, one frosty morning, they couldn't find Horace anywhere, though they all looked—Father and Mother and Grandpa and Grandma and Uncle and Aunty and Milly-Molly-Mandy. But at last, a day or two after, Grandpa was pulling out some hay for the pony Twinkletoes when what do you think he found ? A little ball of prickles cuddled up deep in the hay !

Horace had gone to sleep for the winter, like the proper little hedgehog he was ! (Grandpa said that sort of going to sleep was called ' hibernating.')

So Milly-Molly-Mandy put the hay with the prickly ball inside it into a large box in the barn, with a little bowl of water near by (in case Horace should wake up and want a drink).

And there she left him (sleeping soundly while the cold winds blew and the snows fell) until he should wake up in the spring and come out to play with her again !

(And that's a true story !)

Goes Motoring

III

Milly-Molly-Mandy Goes Motoring

ONCE upon a time Milly-Molly-Mandy had a lovely invitation.

The little girl Jessamine, who lived in the Big House with the iron railings by the cross-roads, came round to the nice white cottage with the thatched roof one Saturday morning to see Milly-Molly-Mandy.

She walked up the path and knocked at the door, and when Milly-Molly-Mandy (who had seen her through the window) ran to open it the little girl Jessamine said, "Hullo, Milly-Molly-Mandy! Mother and I are going in the car to have a picnic on the Downs this afternoon, and Mother says would you like to come too?"

Milly-Molly-Mandy was pleased!

She ran to ask Mother if she might go, and then she ran back to the little girl Jessamine and said, "Mother says thank you very much, I'd love to come!"

So the little girl Jessamine said they would fetch her

Milly-Molly-Mandy

about two o'clock that afternoon. And then she went
back home with a basket of sweet juicy yellow gooseberries, which Father picked for her from his best
gooseberry bushes.

Milly-Molly-Mandy was so excited that she wouldn't
have bothered to eat any dinner at dinner-time, only

Mother said she must, so she did.
And then she put on her hat and
coat, and Aunty lent her a nice
woolly scarf, and Mother saw that
her hair was tidy and that she had
a clean handkerchief. And then just
when she was ready she looked out
of the window and saw the big
motor-car drive up to the gate.

So Milly-Molly-Mandy, in a great
hurry, kissed Father and Mother and
Grandpa and Grandma and Uncle

and Aunty good-bye (she did so wish they could have
been going for a motor-ride too), and then she ran
down the path to the car. And Father and Mother
and Grandpa and Grandma and Uncle and Aunty all
came to the door and waved, and Milly-Molly-Mandy
and Mrs Green and the little girl Jessamine all waved
back from the car.

And then the car went whizzing off, and the nice
white cottage with the thatched roof was out of sight
in a twinkling.

It was such fun to be going to the Downs! Milly-
Molly-Mandy had been taken there once before by Mrs
Green (with little-friend-Susan and Billy Blunt that

time), and she had thought it was just the best place in the whole world for a picnic, so it was very nice to be going there again.

The little girl Jessamine and Milly-Molly-Mandy sat close together in the front seat beside Mrs Green (who drove beautifully), so that they could all see everything and talk about it together.

And they kept on seeing things all the way along. Once a partridge flew out from behind a hedge ; and once a rabbit ran along in front of the car for quite a way ; and once, when they were going very slowly because it was such a pretty lane with so much to see, they saw a little brown moor-hen taking her baby chicks over the road ahead of them ! Mrs Green quietly stopped the car so that they could watch, and the little mother moor-hen hurried across with three babies, and then two more followed her ; and then, after quite a long pause, another little fluffy ball went scurrying across the road in a great hurry, and they all went through a gap in the hedge out of sight.

" He nearly got left behind, didn't he ? " said Mrs Green, starting the car again ; and they went on, all talking about the little moor-hen family out for a walk, and wondering where they were going.

Then presently in the road ahead they saw a bus (not the red bus that passed their village, though). And standing in the road or sitting on the grass by the side

Milly-Molly-Mandy

of the road were a lot of school-children (but none that Milly-Molly-Mandy knew). So Mrs Green had to slow down while they got out of the way.

As they passed they saw that the bus driver was under the bus doing something to the machinery, and the children were looking rather disappointed, and a lady who seemed to be their teacher (but not one from Milly-Molly-Mandy's school) was looking rather worried.

So Mrs Green stopped and called back, " Can we help at all ? "

And the lady who seemed to be their teacher (she was their teacher) came to the side of the car, while all the children crowded round and looked on.

And the lady who was their teacher said they had all been invited to a garden-party, but the bus hired to take them kept on stopping and now it wouldn't move at all, and the lady who was their teacher didn't know quite what to do.

And then one little girl with a little pigtail said in a high little voice, " We've all got our best dresses on for the garden-party, and now we shan't be able to go-o-o ! "

It did seem a pity.

Mrs Green said, " How many are there of you ? "

And the lady who was their teacher said, " Sixteen, including myself."

Then Mrs Green got out and looked at her car and at all the children, and considered things. And Milly-Molly-Mandy and the little girl Jessamine sat and looked at Mrs Green and at all the children, and wondered what could be done about it. And all the children stood

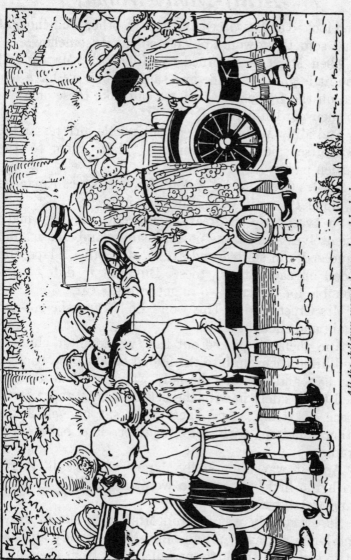

All the children crowded round and looked on

and looked at Mrs Green and at each other, and thought that something would be done about it, somehow.

Then Mrs Green turned to Milly-Molly-Mandy and the little girl Jessamine and said, " Shall we have our tea on the Downs or see if we can take these children to their garden-party ? "

And Milly-Molly-Mandy and the little girl Jessamine of course said (both together), " Take them to the garden-party ! "

So Mrs Green said, " I don't know if we can manage it, but let's see if we can all pack in ! "

So everybody in great excitement tried to make themselves as small as possible, and clambered in and squeezed and shifted and sat in each other's laps and stood on each other's toes. But still it didn't seem possible for the last two to get into the car.

Mrs Green said, " This won't do ! " and she got out again and thought a bit.

And then she picked out the two smallest children and lifted them up into the folded hood at the back of the car, and she and the lady who was their teacher tied them safely in with the belt of a coat and a stout piece of string. And there they sat above all the other children, with toes together, like babes in a cradle !

And it was Milly-Molly-Mandy and the little girl with the little pigtail who were the smallest children (and weren't they just glad !).

So everybody was in, and Mrs Green slowly drove the laden car away ; and Milly-Molly-Mandy and the little girl with the little pigtail waved from their high

Goes Motoring

seat to the bus driver, who stood smiling at them and wiping his oily hands on an oily rag.

Mrs Green drove very slowly and carefully until they came to the big house where the garden-party was to be. And then everybody got out, except Milly-Molly-Mandy and the little girl with the little pigtail, who had to wait to be lifted down.

The lady who was giving the garden-party was very grateful that they had been brought, as she had prepared such a lot of good things for them. And all the children were so grate-ful too that they stood and cheered and cheered and cheered as the car drove off with just Mrs Green and the little girl Jessamine and Milly-Molly-Mandy inside.

" Wasn't that fun ! " said Mrs Green.

" Won't they enjoy their garden-party ! " said the little girl Jessamine.

" Wouldn't it be nice if we could all have ridden in the hood ? " said Milly-Molly-Mandy.

There wasn't time now to go to the Downs for their picnic, but they found a field and spread it out there in the sunshine (and there was a cherry cake with lots of cherries in it !).

And they had such a good time. Milly-Molly-Mandy

thought that field must be the best place in the world, after all, for a picnic ; so it was very nice indeed that they had gone there.

IV

Milly-Molly-Mandy Gets a Surprise

ONCE upon a time, after morning school, Milly-Molly-Mandy saw Mrs Green (the lady who lived in the Big House with the iron railings, which wasn't far from the school) just getting out of her motor-car ; and her little girl Jessamine was with her.

And when the little girl Jessamine saw Milly - Molly - Mandy she said, " Hullo, Milly-Molly-Mandy ! We've just come back from the town. Mother's been to the hairdresser's and had her hair cut off ! "

So when Milly-Molly-Mandy got home to the nice white cottage with the thatched roof, and was having dinner with Father and Mother and Grandpa and Grandma and Uncle and Aunty, she told them the news. And Mother and Grandma and Aunty were quite interested. Mother felt her ' bun,' and said, " I wonder what I should look like with my hair short ! "

Father said, " I like you best as you are."

Gets a Surprise

And Grandpa said, " Nonsense, Polly ! "

And Grandma said, " You'd always have to be going to the barber's."

And Uncle said, " You'll be wanting us to have our beards bobbed next ! "

And Aunty said, " It wouldn't suit you ! "

But Milly-Molly-Mandy said, " Oh, *do*, Mother ! Just like me ! And then you'd look like my sister ! " She looked at Mother carefully, trying to see her with short hair, and added, " I think you'd make a nice sister. DO, Mother ! "

Mother laughed and said, " Oh, it wants a lot of thinking about, Milly-Molly-Mandy ! "

The next evening Mother took a new cream cheese down the road to the Moggs's cottage, and Milly-Molly-Mandy ran with her. And when Mother had given the cream cheese to Mrs Moggs she said, " Mrs Moggs, what do you think about my having my hair off ? "

And when Mrs Moggs had thanked Mother for the cream cheese she said, " Never ! it would be a shame to cut your hair off. I wonder how it would suit me ! "

Mother said, " Let's go and have it done together ! " And Milly-Molly-Mandy said, " Yes, do ! " But Mrs Moggs wouldn't.

It was very windy, and going back up the road again Mother lost her comb, and they couldn't find it as it was getting dark and it was probably in among the grasses under the hedge. So Mother went indoors with her hair quite untidy, and she said, " Now, if I had short hair that would not have happened ! "

Milly-Molly-Mandy

But Father said again, " You're much nicer as you are."

And Grandpa said again, " Nonsense, Polly, you, the mother of a big girl like Milly-Molly-Mandy ! "

But Grandma said, " It would be very comfortable."

And Uncle said, " You can always grow it again if you want to ! "

And Aunty said, " Well, it wouldn't suit ME ! "

Mother's eyebrows said, " Shall I ? " to Milly-Molly-Mandy, and Milly-Molly-Mandy's head said, " Yes ! " quite decidedly.

The next day Father said he had to drive into the town to buy some gardening tools which he couldn't get at Mr Blunt's shop in the village ; and Mother said she would like to go too. (Milly-Molly-Mandy thought Father and Mother had a sort of smiley look, almost as if they had a little secret between them.)

So Father and Mother drove off in the pony-trap together. And when Milly-Molly-Mandy was walking home from school that afternoon with little-friend-Susan she suddenly began to wonder if Mother was going to have her hair cut off in the town, like the little girl Jessamine's mother did. And she was in such a hurry to get home and see if Mother had come back that as soon as they came to the Moggs's cottage she said "Good-bye" at once to little-friend-Susan, without stopping to look in at her baby sister, or stand and talk or anything, and ran all the rest of the way home.

And when she got into the kitchen there was Mother sitting by the fire making toast for tea ; and Grandma and Aunty were looking at her in an amused sort of way all the time they were putting cups on the table or buttering the toast.

For Mother's hair was short like Milly-Molly-Mandy's ; and she looked so nice, and yet quite motherly still, that Milly-Molly-Mandy was as pleased as pleased !

" Has Father seen you ? " she asked. And Mother and Grandma and Aunty all laughed and said, " Yes."

Milly-Molly-Mandy wondered why they laughed quite like that.

Then Mother said, " Ring the bell outside the back door, Milly-Molly-Mandy, to tell the men-folk tea is ready." So Milly-Molly-Mandy rang the bell loudly, and she could hear the men-folk's voices round by the barn. She wondered what they were laughing at.

Then everybody sat down to tea, and Milly-Molly-Mandy couldn't keep her eyes off Mother's hair. Mother looked so nice, and sort of smiley ; Milly-Molly-Mandy couldn't think what she was smiling at so, as she put sugar in the cups. Uncle looked sort of smiley, too, down in his beard—everybody was looking sort of smiley !

Milly-Molly-Mandy looked round the table in surprise.

Milly-Molly-Mandy was satisfied

Gets a Surprise

And then she saw there was a strange man sitting
in Father's place ! And she was so surprised that she
stared hard, while everybody watched her and laughed
outright.

And then Mother patted her shoulder, and said,
"Wasn't Father naughty ? He went and had his beard
cut off while I was having my hair
done ! "

And the 'strange man' who was
Father stroked his chin, and said,
"Don't you think I look very nice
shingled too, Milly-Molly-Mandy ? "

It was quite a long time before
Milly-Molly-Mandy was able to say
anything. And then she wanted to know what Father
and Mother thought of each other.

And Father said, " I told you before, I like her best
just as she is—so I do ! "

And Mother said, " I'll like him best as he is—when
I get used to it ! "

And when Milly-Molly-Mandy had tried how it felt
kissing Father without his beard she said in a satisfied
way, " I think everybody's nicest as they are, really,
aren't they ? "

And Aunty, poking a hairpin back in her own hair,
quite agreed.

Milly-Molly-Mandy

V

Milly-Molly-Mandy Goes on an Expedition

ONCE upon a time it was a Monday-bank-holiday
Milly-Molly-Mandy had been looking forward to
this Monday-bank-holiday for a long time, more than
a week, for she and Billy Blunt had been planning to

go for a long fishing expedition
on that day.

It was rather exciting.

They were to get up very early
and take their dinners with them
and their rods and lines and jam-
jars, and go off all on their own
along by the brook, and not be
back until quite late in the day.

Milly-Molly-Mandy went to bed
the night before with all the things
she wanted for the expedition
arranged beside her bed—a new little tin mug (to drink
out of), and a bottle (for drinking-water), and a large
packet of bread-and-butter and an egg and a banana
(for her dinner), and a jam-jar (to carry the fish in),
and a little green fishing net (to catch them with), and
some string and a safety-pin (which it is always useful
to have), and her school satchel (to put things in).
For when you are going off for the whole day you
want quite a lot of things with you.

When Milly-Molly-Mandy woke up on Monday-bank-

36

Goes on an Expedition

holiday morning she thought to herself, " Oh, dear ! it is a grey sort of day—I do hope it isn't going to rain ! "

But anyhow she knew she was going to enjoy herself, and she jumped up and washed and dressed and put on her hat and the satchel strap over her shoulder.

And then the sunshine came creeping over the trees outside, and Milly-Molly-Mandy saw that it had only been a grey day because she was up before the sun—and she felt a sort of little skip inside, because she was so very sure she was going to enjoy herself !

Just then there came a funny gritty sound like a handful of earth on the window-pane, and when she put her head out there was Billy Blunt, eating a large piece of bread-and-butter and grinning up at her, looking very businesslike with rod and line and jam-jar and bulging satchel.

Milly-Molly-Mandy called out of the window in a loud whisper, " Isn't it a lovely day ? I'm just coming ! "

And Billy Blunt called back in a loud whisper, " Come on ! Hurry up ! It's getting late."

So Milly-Molly-Mandy hurried up like anything, and picked up her things and ran creeping downstairs, past Father's and Mother's room, and Grandpa's and Grandma's room, and Uncle's and Aunty's room. And she filled her bottle at the tap in the scullery, and took up the thick slice of bread-and-butter which Mother had left between two plates ready for her breakfast, and unlocked the back door and slipped out into the fresh morning air.

And there they were, off on their Monday-bank-holiday expedition !

" Isn't it lovely ! " said Milly-Molly-Mandy, with a little hop.

" Umm ! Come on ! " said Billy Blunt.

So they went out of the back gate and across the meadow to the brook, walking very businesslikely and enjoying their bread-and-butter very thoroughly.

" We'll go that way," said Billy Blunt, " because that's the way we don't generally go."

" And when we come to a nice place we'll fish," said Milly-Molly-Mandy.

" But that won't be for a long way yet," said Billy Blunt.

So they went on walking very businesslikely (they had eaten their bread-and-butter by this time) until they had left the nice white cottage with the thatched roof a long way behind, and the sun was shining down quite hotly.

" It seems like a real expedition when you have the whole day to do it in, doesn't it ? " said Milly-Molly-Mandy. " I wonder what the time is now ! "

" Not time for dinner yet," said Billy Blunt. " But I could eat it."

" So could I," said Milly-Molly-Mandy. " Let's have a drink of water." So they each had a little tin mugful of water, and drank it very preciously to make it last, as the bottle didn't hold much.

Off on their Monday-bank-holiday expedition!

Milly-Molly-Mandy

The brook was too muddy and weedy for drinking, but it was a very interesting brook. One place, where it had got rather blocked up, was just full of tadpoles—they caught ever so many with their hands and put them in the jam-jars, and watched them swim about and wiggle their little black tails and open and shut their little black mouths. Then farther on were lots of stepping-stones in the stream, and Milly-Molly-Mandy and Billy Blunt had a fine time scrambling about from one to another.

Billy Blunt slipped once, with one foot into the water, so he took off his boots and socks and tied them round his neck. And it looked so nice that Milly-Molly-Mandy took off one boot and sock and tried it too. But the water and the stones were *so-o* cold that she put them on again, and just tried to be fairly careful how she went. But even so she slipped once, and caught her frock on a branch and pulled the button off, and had to fasten it together with a safety-pin. (So wasn't it a good thing she had brought one with her?)

Presently they came to a big flat mossy stone beside the brook. And Milly-Molly-Mandy said, " That's where we ought to eat our dinners, isn't it ? I wonder what the time is now ! "

Billy Blunt looked round and considered ; and then he said, " Somewhere about noon, I should say. Might think about eating soon, as we had breakfast early. Less to carry, too."

And Milly-Molly-Mandy said, " Let's spread it out all ready, anyhow ! It's a lovely place here."

So they laid the food out on the flat stone, with the

Goes on an Expedition

bottle of water and little tin mug in the middle, and it looked so good and they felt so hungry that, of course, they just had to set to and eat it all up straight away.

And it *did* taste nice!

And the little black tadpoles in the glass jam-jars beside them swam round and round, and wiggled their little black tails and opened and shut their little black mouths; till at last Milly-Molly-Mandy said, " We've taken them away from their dinners, haven't we? Let's put them back now."

And Billy Blunt said, " Yes. We'll want the pots for real fishes soon."

So they emptied the tadpoles back into the brook, where they wiggled away at once to their meals.

" Look! There's a fish!" cried Milly-Molly-Mandy, pointing. And Billy Blunt hurried and fetched his rod and line, and settled to fishing in real earnest.

Milly-Molly-Mandy went a little farther downstream, and poked about with her net in the water; and soon she caught a fish, and put it in her jam-jar, and ran to show it to Billy Blunt. And Billy Blunt said, " Huh!" But he said it wasn't proper fishing without a rod and line, so it didn't really count.

But Milly-Molly-Mandy liked it quite well that way, all the same.

So they fished and they fished along the banks, and sometimes they saw quite big fish, two or three inches long, and Billy Blunt got quite excited and borrowed

Milly-Molly-Mandy

Milly-Molly-Mandy's net ; and they got quite a number of fish in their jam-jars.

" Oh, don't you wish we'd brought our teas too, so we could stay here a long, long time ? " said Milly-Molly-Mandy.

" Umm," said Billy Blunt.  " We ought to have done. Expect we'll have to be getting back soon."

So at last as they got hungry, and thirsty too (having finished all the bottle of water), they began to pack up their things, and Billy Blunt put on his socks and boots. And they tramped all the way back, scrambling up and down the banks, and jumping the stepping-stones.

When they got near home Milly-Molly-Mandy said doubtfully, " What about our fishes ? "

And Billy Blunt said, " We don't really want 'em now, do we ? We only wanted a fishing expedition." So they counted how many there were (there were fifteen), and then emptied them back into the brook, where they darted off at once to their meals.

And Milly-Molly-Mandy and Billy Blunt went on up through the meadow to the nice white cottage with the thatched roof, feeling very hungry, and hoping they weren't too badly late for tea.

And when they got in Father and Mother and Grandpa

Helps to Thatch a Roof

nd Grandma and Uncle and Aunty were all sitting at
able, just finishing—what DO you think?

Why, their midday dinner!

Milly-Molly-Mandy and Billy Blunt couldn't think
ow it had happened. But when you get up so very
arly to go on fishing expeditions, and get so very
ungry, well, it *is* rather difficult to reckon the time
properly!

VI

Milly-Molly-Mandy Helps to Thatch a Roof

ONCE upon a time it was a very blustery night,
so very blustery that it woke Milly-Molly-Mandy
ight up several times.

Milly-Molly-Mandy's
ittle attic bedroom was
ust under the thatched
oof, so she could hear
he wind blowing in
he thatch, as well as
attling her little low
window, and even shak-
ng her door.

Milly - Molly - Mandy
ad to pull the bed-
clothes well over her
ars to shut out some of the noise before she could
o to sleep at all, and so did Father and Mother and
Grandpa and Grandma and Uncle and Aunty, in their
bedrooms. It was so very blustery.

43

Milly-Molly-Mandy

The next morning, when Milly-Molly-Mandy wok[e] up properly, the wind was still very blustery, thoug[h] it didn't sound quite so loud as it did in the dark.

Milly-Molly-Mandy sat up in her little bed, thinking "What a noisy night it was!" And she looked towar[d] her little low window to see if it wer[e] raining.

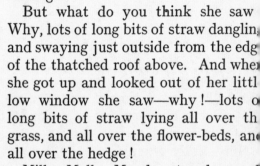

But what do you think she saw[?] Why, lots of long bits of straw danglin[g] and swaying just outside from the edg[e] of the thatched roof above. And whe[n] she got up and looked out of her littl[e] low window she saw—why!—lots o[f] long bits of straw lying all over th[e] grass, and all over the flower-beds, an[d] all over the hedge!

Milly-Molly-Mandy stared round[,] thinking, "It's been raining stra[w] in the night!"

And then she thought some more. And suddenly sh[e] said right out loud, "Ooh! the wind's blowing our nic[e] thatched roof off!"

And then Milly-Molly-Mandy didn't wait to thin[k] any longer, but ran barefooted down into Father's an[d] Mother's room, calling out, "Ooh! Father and Mother[,] the wind's blowing our nice thatched roof off, and it'[s] lying all over the garden!"

Then Father jumped out of bed, and put his boot[s] on his bare feet, and his big coat over his pyjamas, an[d] ran outside to look. And Mother jumped out of bed[,] and wrapped the down-quilt round Milly-Molly-Mandy[,] and went with her to the window to look (but there wasn't anything to see from there).

Then Father came back to say that one corner of the thatched roof was being blown off, and it would have to be seen to immediately before it got any worse. And then everybody began to get dressed.

Milly-Molly-Mandy thought it was kind of funny to have breakfast just the same as usual while the roof was blowing off. She felt very excited about it, and ate her porridge nearly all up before she even remembered beginning it !

" When shall you see to the roof ? " asked Milly-Molly-Mandy. " Directly after breakfast ? "

And Father said, " Yes, it must be seen to as soon as possible."

" How will you see to it ? " asked Milly-Molly-Mandy. " With a long ladder ? "

And Father said, " No, it's too big a job for me. We must send to Mr Critch the Thatcher, and he'll bring a long ladder and mend it."

Milly-Molly-Mandy felt sorry that Father couldn't mend it himself, but it would be nice to see Mr Critch the Thatcher mend it.

Directly after breakfast Aunty put on her hat and coat to go down to the village with the message ; and Milly-Molly-Mandy put on her hat and coat and went with her, because she wanted to see where Mr Critch the Thatcher lived. And as they went out of the gate the wind got another bit of thatch loose on the roof, and blew it down at them ; so they hurried as fast as

Milly-Molly-Mandy

they could, along the white road with the hedges each side, down to the village.

But when Aunty knocked at Mr Critch the Thatcher's door (he lived in one of the little cottages just by the pond where the ducks were), Mrs Critch, the Thatcher's

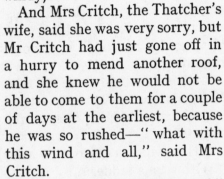

wife, opened it (and her apron blew about like a flag, it was so windy).

And Mrs Critch, the Thatcher's wife, said she was very sorry, but Mr Critch had just gone off in a hurry to mend another roof, and she knew he would not be able to come to them for a couple of days at the earliest, because he was so rushed—"what with this wind and all," said Mrs Critch.

"Dear, dear!" said Aunty. "Whatever shall we do?"

Mrs Critch was sorry, but she did not know what they could do, except wait until Mr Critch could come.

"Dear, dear!" said Aunty. "And meantime our roof will be getting worse and worse." Then Aunty and Milly-Molly-Mandy said good morning to Mrs Critch, and went out through her little gate into the road again.

"Father will have to mend it now, won't he, Aunty?" said Milly-Molly-Mandy.

"It isn't at all easy to thatch a roof," said Aunty. "You have to know how. I wonder what we can do!"

They set off back home along the white road with the hedges each side, and Aunty said, "Well, there must be

Helps to Thatch a Roof

a way out, somehow." And Milly-Molly-Mandy said,
" I expect Father will know what to do." So they
hurried along, holding their hats on.

, As they passed the Moggs's cottage they saw little-
friend-Susan trying to hang a towel on the line, with
the wind trying all the time to wrap her up in it.

Milly-Molly-Mandy called out, " Hullo, Susan ! Our
roof's being blown off, and Mr Critch the Thatcher
can't come and mend it, so Father will have to. Do
you want to come and see ? " Little-friend-Susan was
very interested, and as soon as she had got the towel
up she came along with them.

When Father and Mother and Grandpa and Grandma
and Uncle heard their news they all looked as if they
were saying " Dear, dear ! " to themselves. But Milly-
Molly-Mandy looked quite pleased, and said, " Now
you'll have to mend the roof, won't you, Father ? "

And Father looked at Uncle, and said, " Well, Joe.
How about it ? " And Uncle said, " Right, John ! " in
his big voice.

And then Father and Uncle buttoned their jackets
(so that the wind shouldn't flap them), and fetched
ladders (to reach the roof with), and a rake (to comb
the straw tidy with), and wooden pegs (with which to
fasten it down). And then they put one ladder so that
they could climb up *to* the thatched roof, and another
ladder with hooks on the end so that they could climb
up *on* the thatched roof ; and then Father gathered up
a big armful of straw, and he and Uncle set to work
busily to mend the hole in the thatch as well as they
could, till Mr Critch the Thatcher could come.

Milly-Molly-Mandy

Milly-Molly-Mandy and little-friend-Susan, down below, set to work busily to collect the straw from the hedges and the flower-beds and the grass, piling it up in one corner, ready for Father when he came down for another armful. And they helped to hold the ladder steady, and handed up sticks for making the pattern

round the edge of the thatch, and fetched things that Father or Uncle called out for, and were very useful indeed.

Soon the roof began to look much better.

Then Father fetched a big pair of shears, and he snip-snip-snipped the straggly ends of the straw all round Milly-Molly-Mandy's little bedroom window, up under the roof. (Milly-Molly-Mandy thought it was just like the nice white cottage having its hair cut !) And then Father and Uncle stretched a big piece of wire netting over the mended place, and fastened it down with pegs. (Milly-Molly-Mandy thought it was just like the nice white cottage having a hair-net put on and fastened with hairpins !)

And then the roof was all trim and tidy again, and

48

Soon the roof began to look much better

they wouldn't feel in any sort of a hurry for Mr Critch the Thatcher to come and thatch it properly.

" Isn't it a lovely roof ? " said Milly-Molly-Mandy. " I knew Father could do it ! "

" Well, you can generally manage to do a thing when you have to, Milly-Molly-Mandy," said Father ; but he looked quite pleased with himself, and so did Uncle.

And when they saw what a nice snug roof they had now so did Mother and Grandpa and Grandma and Aunty and Milly-Molly-Mandy !

VII

Milly-Molly-Mandy Writes Letters

ONCE upon a time Milly-Molly-Mandy heard the postman's knock, bang-BANG ! on the front door ; so she ran hop-skip down the passage to look in the letter-box, because she always sort of hoped there might be a letter for her !

But there wasn't.

" I do wish the postman would bring me a letter sometimes," said Milly-Molly-Mandy, coming slowly back into the kitchen. " He never does. There's only a business-looking letter for Father and an advertisement for Uncle."

And then Milly-Molly-Mandy noticed that the business-looking letter was from Holland (where Father got his flower bulbs) and had a Dutch stamp on it, so that was more interesting. Milly-Molly-Mandy was

Writes Letters

collecting foreign stamps. She had collected one Irish one already, and it was stuck in Billy Blunt's new stamp album. (Billy Blunt had just started collecting stamps, so Milly-Molly-Mandy was collecting for him.)

" If you want the postman to bring you letters you'll have to write them to other people first," said Mother, putting the letters up on the mantelshelf till Father and Uncle should come in.

" But I haven't got any stamps," said Milly-Molly-Mandy.

" I'll give you one when you want it," said Grandma, pulling the kettle forward on the stove.

" But I don't know who to write to," said Milly-Molly-Mandy.

"You'll have to think round a little," said Aunty, clearing her sewing off the table.

" There's only Billy Blunt and little-friend-Susan, and it would be silly to write to them when I see them every day," said Milly-Molly-Mandy.

" We must just think," said Mother, spreading the cloth on the table for tea. " There are sure to be lots of people who would like to have letters by post, as well as you."

Milly-Molly-Mandy

Milly-Molly-Mandy hadn't thought of that. "Do you suppose they'd run like anything to the letter-box because they thought there might be a letter from me?" she said. "What fun! I've got the fancy notepaper that Aunty gave me at Christmas—they'll like that, won't they? Who *can* I write to?"

And then she helped to lay the table, and made a piece of toast at the fire for Grandma; and presently

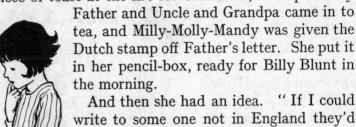

Father and Uncle and Grandpa came in to tea, and Milly-Molly-Mandy was given the Dutch stamp off Father's letter. She put it in her pencil-box, ready for Billy Blunt in the morning.

And then she had an idea. "If I could write to some one not in England they'd stick foreign stamps on their letters when they wrote back, wouldn't they?"

And then Aunty had an idea. "Why, there are my little nieces in America!" she said. (For Aunty had a brother who went to America when he was quite young, and now he had three little children, whom none of them had seen or knew hardly anything about, for "Tom," as Aunty called him, wasn't a very good letter writer, and only wrote to her sometimes at Christmas.)

"Ooh, yes!" said Milly-Molly-Mandy, "and I don't believe Billy has an American stamp yet. What are their names, Aunty? I forget."

"Sallie and Lallie," said Aunty, "and the boy is Tom, after my brother, but they call him Buddy. They would like to have a letter from their cousin in England, I'm sure."

Writes Letters

So Milly-Molly-Mandy looked out the box of fancy notepaper that Aunty had given her, and kept it by her side while she did her home-lessons after tea. And then, when she had done them all, she wrote quite a long letter to her cousin Sallie (at least it looked quite a long letter, because the pink notepaper was rather small), telling about her school, and her friends, and

Billy Blunt's collection, and about Toby the dog, and Topsy the cat, and what Father and Mother and Grandpa and Grandma and Uncle and Aunty were all doing at that moment in the kitchen, and outside in the barn ; so that Sallie should get to know them all. And then there was just room to send her love to Lallie and Buddy, and to sign her name.

It was quite a nice letter.

Milly-Molly-Mandy showed it to Mother and Aunty, and then (just to make it more interesting) she put in a piece of coloured silver paper and two primroses (the first she had found that year), and stuck down the flap of the pink envelope.

The next morning she posted her letter in the red pillar-box on the way to school (little-friend-Susan was quite interested when she showed her the address) ; and then she tried to forget all about it, because she knew

it would take a long while to get there and a longer
while still for an answering letter to come back.

After morning school she gave the Dutch stamp to
Billy Blunt for his collection. He said he had got one,
as they were quite common, but that it might come in
useful for exchanging with some other fellow. And after
school that very afternoon he told her he had exchanged
it for a German stamp; so it was very useful.

" Have you got an American stamp ? " asked Milly-
Molly-Mandy.

" No," said Billy Blunt. " What I want to get hold
of is a Czecho-Slovakian one. Ted Smale's just got
one. His uncle gave it to him."

Milly-Molly-Mandy didn't think she could ever collect
such a stamp as that for Billy Blunt, but she was glad
he hadn't got an American one yet.

All that week and the next Milly-Molly-Mandy rushed
to the letter-box every time she heard the postman,
although she knew there wouldn't be an answer for
about three weeks, anyhow. But the postman's knock,
bang-BANG! sounded so exciting she always forgot to
remember in time.

A whole month went by, and Milly-Molly-Mandy
began almost to stop expecting a letter at all, or at
least one from abroad.

And then one day she came home after school a bit
later than usual, because she and little-friend-Susan
had been picking wind-flowers and primroses under a
hedge, very excited to think spring had really come.
But when she did get in what DO you think she found
waiting for her, on her plate at the table ?

They sat and wrote letters together

Milly-Molly-Mandy

Why, *three* letters, just come by post! One from Sallie, one from Lallie, and one from Buddy!

They were so pleased at having a letter from England

 that they had all written back, hoping she would write again. And they sent some snapshots of themselves, and Buddy enclosed a Japanese stamp for Billy Blunt's collection.

The next Saturday Billy Blunt came to tea with Milly-Molly-Mandy and she gave him the four stamps, three American and one Japanese. And, though he said they were not really valuable ones, he was as pleased as anything to have them!

And when the table was cleared they sat and wrote letters together — Milly-Molly-Mandy to Sallie and Lallie, and Billy Blunt to Buddy (to thank him for the stamp), with a little P.S. from Milly-Molly-Mandy (to thank him for his letter).

Milly-Molly-Mandy does like letter-writing, because now she has got three more friends!

VIII

Milly-Molly-Mandy Learns to Ride

ONCE upon a time, when Milly-Molly-Mandy had gone down to the village to get some things for Mother at the grocer's shop, she saw Miss Muggins's little niece Jilly wheeling a bicycle out of their side door.

Learns to Ride

It was a young bicycle, not a grown-up one, and it was very new, and very shiny, and very black-and-silvery.

"Hullo!" said Milly-Molly-Mandy, looking at it interestedly, "is that your bicycle?"

"Hullo!" said Miss Muggins's Jilly, trying to look as if nothing unusual were happening. "Yes. My uncle gave it to me."

"Can you ride it?" asked Milly-Molly-Mandy.

"Oh, yes," said Miss Muggins's Jilly, "I ride it up and down the road. I'm just going to do it now. Good-bye." And

she got up on it and rode off (rather wobblily, but still she did it) toward the cross-roads.

Milly-Molly-Mandy went into the grocer's shop with her basket, wishing she could have a ride, but of course as it was such a beautiful new bicycle she hadn't liked to ask.

When she came out again Miss Muggins's Jilly passed her, riding back; and she got off when she came to the letter-box at the corner to turn round, because she couldn't ride round without toppling over yet.

Milly-Molly-Mandy couldn't help saying to her longingly, "I do wish I could have a little ride on it."

But Miss Muggins's Jilly said, "I don't expect you could if you've never learned—you'd fall off. And my

Milly-Molly-Mandy

Aunty says I've got to be very careful with it, because it's new. I'm going to ride back to the cross-roads now. Good-bye." And Miss Muggins's Jilly rode off again, and Milly-Molly-Mandy walked on homeward.

As she passed the duck-pond she saw Billy Blunt hanging over the rail to see if he could see a tiddler.

And Milly-Molly-Mandy said, " Hullo, Billy ? What do you think ? Jilly's got a new bicycle ! "

And Billy Blunt said, " I know. I've seen it."

" I wish we had bicycles, don't you ? " said Milly-Molly-Mandy.

" I have got one," said Billy Blunt surprisingly.

" You haven't ! " said Milly-Molly-Mandy.

" I've got two, if I wanted 'em," said Billy Blunt.

" Where are they ? " asked Milly-Molly-Mandy.

" In our shed," said Billy Blunt.

" I don't believe it ! " said Milly-Molly-Mandy. " You're only funning. Because you'd ride them if you had them—only you wouldn't have two, anyhow ! "

But Billy Blunt only grinned ; and Milly-Molly-Mandy walked on homeward.

As she passed the Moggs's cottage she saw little-friend-Susan on the other side of the wall playing with her baby sister. And Milly-Molly-Mandy said, " Hullo, Susan ? What do you think ? Jilly's got a new bicycle ! "

Learns to Ride

" Oh ! " said little-friend-Susan, " I wish we'd got bicycles."

And Milly-Molly-Mandy said, " I wish we could ride, anyhow—then p'r'aps Jilly would let us have a tiny little ride on hers." And then Milly-Molly-Mandy walked on home to the nice white cottage with the thatched roof and gave Mother her basket of groceries.

A few days later, coming home from school in the afternoon (Miss Muggins's Jilly had just gone in at Miss Muggins's side door, which they passed first), Billy Blunt stopped as he was going in at the little white gate by the corn-shop, and said to Milly-Molly-Mandy and little-friend-Susan, " Want to see something ? "

Milly-Molly-Mandy and little-friend-Susan of course said " Yes ! " at once.

And Billy Blunt said, " Come on and see ! "

So Milly-Molly-Mandy and little-friend-Susan went with him through the little white gate into the Blunts' garden.

" What is it ? " asked Milly-Molly-Mandy. But Billy Blunt only led the way to the old shed at the farther end. " Oh, I know ! " said Milly-Molly-Mandy, with a sudden guess. " It's your old bicycles—but I don't believe it ! "

Billy Blunt solemnly undid the rickety door of the shed and pulled it open. " There you are, Miss ! " he said, grinning triumphantly. " Now you can just unsay what you said."

And there in the dusty, mouldy-smelling shed, among a lot of boxes and bottles and paint-tins and other lumber, stood two old bicycles leaning against the wall.

59

They were covered all over with rust and cobwebs, and their tyres were falling off in rags.

" Oh-h-h ! " said Milly-Molly-Mandy and little-friend-Susan together, pushing in closer to look.

" They aren't any good," said little-friend-Susan disappointedly.

" Oh, wait ! They might be ! Can't we make them be ? " cried Milly-Molly-Mandy excitedly.

Billy Blunt wheeled one of the bicycles out—only it wouldn't wheel because the wheels were all rusty. Milly-Molly-Mandy pulled the other one out ; it was a lady's bike, and just a bit smaller (and it did make her hands dirty !).

" Oh, Billy ! " said Milly-Molly-Mandy, " if we could only make the wheels go round you could learn on that one and we could learn on this one. What fun ! "

And little-friend-Susan said, " Oh, we never could, but let's try ! " and she pulled a whole mass of cobwebs off the spokes, and jumped as a big black spider ran away.

Billy Blunt put his cap and school satchel down on the grass, and started poking and scraping with a bit of stick to loosen the rust. And then the others started working the wheels backward and forward to make them turn. And they pulled off the ragged tyres in strips, and rubbed at the rust with bunches of grass ; and they DID get dirty, all red rusty dirt ! (But they enjoyed it !)

They forgot all about tea till Mrs Blunt called Billy Blunt in ; then Milly-Molly-Mandy and little-friend-Susan ran off to their homes, promising to come back directly after.

Learns to Ride

Milly-Molly-Mandy ate her tea as quickly as she could, talking about bicycles all the time ; and Mother made her take an old overall to put on, and gave her a bundle of rags with which to rub the rust and dust off. And then she ran down the road to little-friend-Susan's, and the two of them ran along together back to the Blunts' garden.

Billy Blunt was already hard at work again with an old kitchen knife and an oil-can, and he had got one wheel to go round quite nicely. They were pleased !

Then the three had a real set-to, scraping and rubbing and oiling (and chattering) until it got quite dusk, and Mrs Blunt came out and said they must run along home to bed now.

The next day, after school, they wheeled the two bikes (making such a rattle !) on to the waste ground at the back of Mr Blunt's corn-shop, where the grass was nice and soft for falling on (or at any rate softer than the road !). And there they started to practise cycling—Billy Blunt on the gentleman's bicycle, and Milly-Molly-Mandy and little-friend-Susan taking turns riding and holding each other up on the lady's bicycle. (Mr Blunt had hammered the saddles down for them as low as they would go.)

It was fun !

Milly-Molly-Mandy

And what a rattling, scraping, creaking noise they did make, to be sure, over the grass! And how they did keep on toppling over sideways, and calling to each other to hold them up, and falling with a crash among the buttercups! And how they did scratch and scrape and bump themselves! And HOW they did enjoy it all!

By the end of the evening Billy Blunt could ride half as far as the tree before he fell off, and Milly-Molly-Mandy and little-friend-Susan could do nearly as well (but of course they had to take turns, which made them a bit slower).

Milly-Molly-Mandy could hardly wait for the night to go, she was so keen to get back to her riding!

It was Saturday, next day, so they were able to spend nearly all day in the field, rattling and bumping round over the tufty grass and the molehills. And presently they started riding up and down the path by the forge, where it was easier going, only harder if you fell off (but they didn't fall off so much now).

Mr Rudge the Blacksmith laughed at them as they rattled past the open door of the forge, where he was clanging away with his big hammer; but they didn't mind. Billy Blunt even managed to wave to him once without falling off!

Miss Muggins's Jilly came and watched them for a while. And presently she said, "You are riding

What a rattling, scraping, creaking noise they did make!

nicely! I'll let you have a ride on my bicycle soon, Milly-Molly-Mandy."

Milly-Molly-Mandy thanked her very much, and thought it would be nice to know how it felt to be on a real bicycle. But all the same, she couldn't help thinking that no bicycle in the whole world could be *half* as thrilling to ride on as these rusty, rattling, creaking old bikes of Billy Blunt's!

IX

Milly-Molly-Mandy Makes a Garden

ONCE upon a time Milly-Molly-Mandy was very excited.

There was to be a grand Flower and Vegetable Show in the village in a month's time (the posters telling about it were stuck on the back of the forge); and besides prizes being given for all the usual things—such as the finest potatoes and strawberries and garden flowers, and the best home-made jams and pickles—there were also to be prizes for the prettiest posy of wild flowers, and the best miniature garden (grown in a bowl).

" Ooh ! " said Milly-Molly-Mandy to little-friend-Susan (they were reading the poster together after morning school) ; " I wonder ! "

" What ? " said little-friend-Susan.

" I wonder," said Milly-Molly-Mandy, " if I shall grow a little garden in a bowl, and send it to the Flower Show ! "

" Oh, could you ? " said little-friend-Susan. " And do

Makes a Garden

you suppose I could make a posy and send it in too?
Wouldn't it be lovely to win a prize?"

"I don't suppose we could," said Milly-Molly-Mandy,
"but it would be such
fun to try. I'm going
to ask Mother."

So when Milly-Molly-
Mandy got home she
asked if she might
make a little garden
and send it to the
Flower Show. And
Mother said, "If you
can make it nicely
enough you may, Milly-
Molly-Mandy. Father
is going to send in some
of his best gooseberries,
and I am going to send
some pots of jam and

pickles; so we shall make a good showing, all together!"

Then Mother got out a brown pottery pie-dish from
the kitchen cupboard and asked Milly-Molly-Mandy if
she thought that would do to grow her garden in; and
after Milly-Molly-Mandy had considered it well she
thought it would. She put some broken bits of flower-
pot at the bottom (to help to drain off the wet), and then
she filled the dish with the brownest, softest earth she
could find. And then she had to think what to plant in
her garden so that it would look just like a real big one,
if it weren't so very little!

Milly-Molly-Mandy

It took a lot of thinking.

After school Milly-Molly-Mandy told Billy Blunt about the Flower Show, in case he hadn't heard about it ; but he said he had.

" Are you going to go in for any of the prizes ? " asked Milly-Molly-Mandy.

" Huh ! " was all Billy Blunt said ; but Milly-Molly-Mandy knew he was !

" Which one ? " she asked. And Billy Blunt took her into the old cycle-shed beside the corn-shop and showed her—a fine new red earthenware bowl filled with soft brown earth !

" Billy ! " said Milly-Molly-Mandy. " Fancy your going in for that one ! So am I ! And we can't both win the prize."

" Don't suppose either of us will," said Billy Blunt, " but I mean to have a good try."

" So do I," said Milly-Molly-Mandy.

" And the best one wins," said Billy Blunt.

The next day Milly-Molly-Mandy set the first plant in her garden. It was a tiny little holly-tree, which she had found growing almost in the path under the big holly-tree by the hedge. (It had grown from one of the fallen berries.) Milly-Molly-Mandy knew it would only be trodden on if left there, so she carefully dug it up and planted it in the soft brown earth in her bowl.

Next she went poking about down by the brook, and she found some nice moss-grown bits of rotten wood ; one bit looked just like a little green mossy cave, so she took it home and put it in the bowl by the holly-tree ; and then she planted some grass and a daisy root

Showed her a fine new red earthenware bowl

Milly-Molly-Mandy

in. the rest of the space, and it really looked quite a pretty garden. It grew so nicely, and the baby holly-tree opened out its new little leaves as if it felt quite at home there.

Billy Blunt wouldn't let anyone see his garden until he had got it arranged to his liking. And then one day

he said Milly-Molly-Mandy might have a look if she liked. And he fetched it down from his bedroom to show her.

And it was pretty!

There was more room in Billy Blunt's bowl, and he had made it like a rock garden with rough-looking little stones ; and a small sycamore-tree was grow-

ing between them in one place, and a wee sage-bush in another ; and little tiny plants—scarlet pimpernels, and rock-roses, and lady's-bedstraw—sprouted here and there. Milly-Molly-Mandy did like it.

"Oh, Billy!" she said, "yours is much prettier than mine! Except that yours hasn't got a cave in it. You'll get the prize."

But when Billy Blunt saw the mossy cave in Milly-Molly-Mandy's garden he wasn't so sure.

The day of the Flower Show drew near. It was to be held in the village Institute on the Saturday, and everybody who was going to send in (and nearly everybody was) was feeling very busy and important. Mr

68

Makes a Garden

Jakes the Postman had some fine gooseberries and red currants which he meant to enter, and little-friend-Susan said her father and Mrs Green were going to show lots of flowers and vegetables from the garden at the Big House with the iron railings (Mr Moggs was gardener at Mrs Green's), and Mrs Green was making a miniature garden too.

And then, just the very day before the Show (which, of course, was sending-in day), what DO you think happened?

Billy Blunt's little sycamore-tree lost all its leaves! Either he hadn't managed to get all its roots when he dug it up or else it had been left too long in the hot sun, without much earth to grow in; anyhow, when he came back from school there it was, with its leaves all curled up and spoiled.

Billy Blunt was dreadfully disappointed, and so was Milly-Molly-Mandy.

" Whole thing's done for now," said Billy Blunt; " it's nothing without that tree."

" Can't we find another one somewhere? " said Milly-Molly-Mandy. " Let's look! "

" I looked everywhere before I found that one," said Billy Blunt. " Besides, there isn't any time to look. It's got to go in. Only it's no good sending it now."

" Oh, Billy! " said Milly-Molly-Mandy. She was as disappointed as he was. " It won't be any fun sending mine in now. It wouldn't seem fair if I *did* get a prize. But I don't expect it'll get one anyhow—Susan says Mrs Green is sending in a garden."

" Hers won't have a cave in it," said Billy Blunt.

Milly-Molly-Mandy

And then, suddenly, Milly-Molly-Mandy had an idea.

" I tell you what ! Couldn't we make one beautiful garden between us and send it in together ? Why not ? Your big bowl and garden, with my tree and the mossy cave ? Couldn't we ? "

Billy Blunt was very doubtful. " I don't know that we could send in together," he said slowly.

" Why couldn't we ? Mr Moggs and Mrs Green at the Big House do," said Milly-Molly-Mandy. " I'll go and fetch my garden and we'll see how it would look ! "

So she ran all the way home to the nice white cottage with the thatched roof and fetched her little garden ; and then she walked carefully with it all the way back. And what do you think she found Billy Blunt doing ? He was writing a label to see how it would look for the Flower Show : " Sent in by Billy Blunt and Milly-Molly-Mandy."

" Looks quite businesslike," he said. " Did you fetch your tree ? "

The little garden in the pottery dish looked so pretty it almost seemed a pity to spoil it, but Milly-Molly-Mandy insisted. So together they took out the little holly-tree and planted it in place of the sycamore-tree ; and then they arranged the mossy bit of wood at one side of the bowl ; and it all looked so real you almost felt as if you could live in the little green cave, and go clambering on the rocks, or climb the tree, if you wished !

" Well ! " said Milly-Molly-Mandy, sitting back on her heels, " it just couldn't be prettier ! "

" Umm ! " said Billy Blunt, looking very satisfied.

" It's prettier than either of them was before. Let's take it in now."

So they walked across to the Institute and handed in the precious miniature garden, with the sixpence entrance fee between them.

It was so hard to wait till the next day! But on Saturday, as soon as the judges had decided which things had won prizes, the Flower Show was opened and the shilling people could go in. Most people waited till the afternoon, when it cost only sixpence; Father and Mother and Grandpa and Grandma and Uncle  and Aunty and Milly-Molly-Mandy (who was half-price) went then.

The place was filled with people and lovely smells of flowers and strawberries, and there was a great noise of people talking and exclaiming, and cups clattering somewhere at the back, and the village band was tuning up.

Milly-Molly-Mandy could not see Billy Blunt or the miniature gardens; but Father's gooseberries had got first prize, and his basket of vegetables second prize (Mr Moggs's got the first), and Mother had first prize for her jam, but nothing for her marrow-chutney (Mrs Critch, the Thatcher's wife, won that). Little-friend-Susan was there, skipping up and down gleefully because her wild posy had won a third prize.

Milly-Molly-Mandy

And then Milly-Molly-Mandy saw Billy Blunt. He was grinning all over his face!

"Seen the gardens?" he said. "Come on. This way." And he pulled her through the crowd to a table at the farther end, where were arranged several miniature gardens of all sorts and sizes, some of them very pretty ones indeed.

But right in the middle, raised up by itself, was the prettiest one of all; and it was labelled:

' FIRST PRIZE. Sent in by Billy Blunt and Milly-Molly-Mandy ' !

Camps Out

X

Milly-Molly-Mandy Camps Out

ONCE upon a time Milly-Molly-Mandy and Toby the dog went down to the village, to Miss Muggins's shop, on an errand for Mother; and as they passed Mr Blunt's corn-shop Milly-Molly-Mandy saw something new in the little garden at the side. It looked like a small, shabby sort of tent, with a slit in the top and a big checked patch sewn on the side.

Milly-Molly-Mandy wondered what it was doing there. But she didn't see Billy Blunt anywhere about, so she couldn't ask him.

When she came out of Miss Muggins's shop she had another good look over the palings into the Blunts' garden. And while she was looking Billy Blunt came out of their house door with some old rugs and a pillow in his arms.

"Hullo, Billy!" said Milly-Molly-Mandy. "What's that tent-thing?"

"It's a tent," said Billy Blunt, not liking its being called 'thing.'

"But what's it for?" asked Milly-Molly-Mandy.

"It's mine," said Billy Blunt.

"Yours? Your very own? Is it?" said Milly-Molly-Mandy. "Ooh, do let me come and look at it!"

"You can if you want to," said Billy Blunt. "I'm going to sleep in it to-night—camp out."

Milly-Molly-Mandy was very interested indeed. She

73

looked at it well, outside and in. She could only just
stand up in it. Billy Blunt had spread an old mack-
intosh for a ground-sheet, and there was a box in one
corner to hold a bottle of water and a mug, and his
electric torch, and such necessary things ; and when

the front flap of the tent was
closed you couldn't see anything outside, except a tiny
bit of sky and some green
leaves through the tear in
the top.

Milly-Molly-Mandy didn't
want to come out a bit, but
Billy Blunt wanted to put
his bedding in.

" Isn't it beautiful ! Where
did you get it, Billy ? " she
asked.

" My cousin gave it to me,"
said Billy Blunt. " Used
it when he went cycling
holidays. He's got a new one now. I put that patch
on, myself."

Milly-Molly-Mandy thought she could have done it
better ; but still it was quite good for a boy, so she
duly admired it, and offered to mend the other place.
But Billy Blunt didn't think it was worth it, as it would
only tear away again—and he liked a bit of air, anyhow.

" Shan't you feel funny out here all by yourself when
everybody else is asleep ? " said Milly-Molly-Mandy.
" Oh, I wish I had a tent too ! " Then she said good-

bye, and ran with Toby the dog back home to the nice white cottage with the thatched roof, thinking of the tent all the way.

She didn't see little-friend-Susan as she passed the Moggs's cottage along the road ; but when she got as far as the meadow she saw her swinging her baby sister on the big gate.

" Hullo, Milly-Molly-Mandy ! I was just looking for you," said little-friend-Susan, lifting Baby Moggs down. And Milly-Molly-Mandy told her all about Billy Blunt's new tent, and how he was going to sleep out, and how she wished she had a tent too.

Little-friend-Susan was almost as interested as Milly-Molly-Mandy. " Can't we make a tent and play in it in your meadow ? " she said. " It would be awful fun ! "

So they got some bean-poles and bits of sacking from the barn and dragged them down into the meadow. And they had great fun that day trying to make a tent ; only they couldn't get it to stay up properly.

Next morning little-friend-Susan came to play ' tents ' in the meadow again. And this time they tried with an old counterpane, which Mother had given them, and two kitchen chairs ; and they managed to rig up quite a good tent by laying the poles across the chair-backs and draping the counterpane over. They fastened down the spread-out sides with stones ; and the ends, where the chairs were, they hung with sacks. And there they had a perfectly good tent, really quite big enough for two—so long as the two were small, and didn't mind being a bit crowded !

They were just sitting in it, eating apples and

pretending they had no other home to live in, when they heard a " *Hi!* "-ing from the gate ; and when they peeped out there was Billy Blunt, with a great bundle in his arms, trying to get the gate open. So they ran across the grass and opened it for him.

" What have you got ? Is it your tent ? Did you sleep out last night ? " asked Milly-Molly-Mandy.

" Look here," said Billy Blunt, " do you think your father would mind, supposing I pitched my tent in your field ? My folk don't like it in our garden—say it looks too untidy."

Milly-Molly-Mandy was quite sure Father wouldn't mind. So Billy Blunt put the bundle down inside the gate and went off to ask (for of course you never camp anywhere without saying " please " to the owner first). And Father didn't mind a bit, so long as no papers or other rubbish were left about.

Camps Out

So Billy Blunt set up his tent near the others', which was not too far from the nice white cottage with the thatched roof (because it's funny what a long way off from everybody you feel when you've got only a tent round you at night !). And then he went home to fetch his other goods ; and Milly-Molly-Mandy and little-friend-Susan sat in his tent, and wished and wished that their mothers would let them sleep out in the meadow that night.

When Billy Blunt came back with his rugs and things (loaded up on his box on wheels) they asked him if it were very creepy-feeling to sleep out of doors.

And Billy Blunt (having slept out once) said, " Oh, you soon get used to it," and asked why they didn't try it in their tent.

So then Milly-Molly-Mandy and little-friend-Susan looked at each other, and said firmly, " Let's ask ! " So little-friend-Susan went with Milly-Molly-Mandy up to the nice white cottage with the thatched roof, where Mother was just putting a treacle-tart into the oven.

She looked very doubtful when Milly-Molly-Mandy told her what they wanted to do. Then she shut the oven door, and wiped her hands, and said, well, she would just come and look at the tent they had made first. And when she had looked and considered, she said, well, if it were still very fine and dry by the evening perhaps Milly-Molly-Mandy might sleep out there, just for once. And Mother found a rubber ground-sheet and some old blankets and cushions, and gave them to her.

Milly-Molly-Mandy

Then Milly-Molly-Mandy went with little-friend-Susan to the Moggs's cottage, where Mrs Moggs was just putting their potatoes on to boil.

She looked very doubtful at first ; and then she said, well, if Milly-Molly-Mandy's mother had been out to see, and thought it was all right, and if it were a *very*

nice, fine evening, perhaps little-friend-Susan might sleep out, just for once.

So all the rest of that day the three were very busy, making preparations and watching the sky. And when they all went home for supper the evening was beautifully still and warm, and without a single cloud.

So, after supper, they all met together again in the meadow, in the sunset. And they shut and tied up the meadow-gate. (It was all terribly exciting !)

And Mother came out, with Father and Grandpa and Grandma and Uncle and Aunty, to see that all was right, and their ground-sheets well spread under their bedding.

Then little-friend-Susan and Billy Blunt crawled out

Milly-Molly-Mandy

Then Milly-Molly-Mandy and little-friend-Susan crawled into their tent, and Billy Blunt crawled into his tent. And presently Milly-Molly-Mandy crawled out again in her pyjamas, and ran about with bare feet on the grass with Toby the dog ; and then little-friend-Susan and Billy Blunt, in their pyjamas, crawled out and ran about too (because it feels so very nice, and so

sort of new, to be running about under the sky in your pyjamas !).

And Father and Mother and Grandpa and Grandma and Uncle and Aunty laughed, and looked on as if they wouldn't mind doing it too, if they weren't so grown up.

Then Mother said, " Now I think it's time you campers popped into bed. Good night ! " And they went off home.

So Milly-Molly-Mandy and little-friend-Susan called " Good night ! " and crawled into one tent, and Billy Blunt caught Toby the dog and crawled into the other.

And the trees outside grew slowly blacker and blacker until they couldn't be seen at all ; and the owls hooted ; and a far-away cow moo-ed ; and now and then Toby the dog wuffed, because he thought he heard a rabbit ; and sometimes Milly-Molly-Mandy or little-friend-Susan squeaked, because they thought they felt a spider walking on them. And once Billy Blunt called out to ask if they were still awake, and they said they were, and was he? and he said of course he was.

And then at last they all fell fast asleep.

And in no time at all the sun was shining through their tents, telling them to wake up and come out, because it was the next day.

And Billy Blunt and Milly-Molly-Mandy and little-friend-Susan DID enjoy that camping-out night!

XI

Milly-Molly-Mandy Keeps House

ONCE upon a time Milly-Molly-Mandy was left one evening in the nice white cottage with the thatched roof to keep house.

There was something called a political meeting being held in the next village (Milly-Molly-Mandy didn't know quite what that meant, but it was something to do with voting, which was something you had to do when you grew up), and Father and Mother and Grandpa and Grandma and Uncle and Aunty all thought they ought to go to it.

Milly-Molly-Mandy said she would not mind one bit being left, especially if she could have little-friend-Susan in to keep her company.

So Mother said, "Very well, then, Milly-Molly-Mandy, we'll have little-friend-Susan in to keep you company. And you needn't open the door if anyone knocks unless you know who it is. And I'll leave you out

some supper, in case we may be a little late getting
back."

Little-friend-Susan was only too pleased to come and
spend the evening with Milly-Molly-Mandy. So after

tea she came in; and then
Father and Mother and
Grandpa and Grandma and
Uncle and Aunty put on
their hats and coats, and
said good-bye, and went off.

And Milly-Molly-Mandy
and little-friend-Susan
shut the door carefully
after them, and there they
were, all by themselves,
keeping house!

"What fun!" said little-
friend-Susan. "What'll we
do?"

"Well," said Milly-
Molly-Mandy, "if we're
housekeepers I think we ought to wear aprons."

So they each tied on one of Mother's aprons.

And then little-friend-Susan said, "Now, if we've got
aprons on we ought to work."

So Milly-Molly-Mandy fetched a dustpan and brush
and swept up some crumbs from the floor; and little-
friend-Susan folded the newspaper that was lying all anyhow by Grandpa's chair and put it neatly on the shelf.
And then they banged the cushions and straightened
the chairs, feeling very housekeeperish indeed.

Keeps House

Then little-friend-Susan looked at the plates of bread-and-dripping on the table, with the jug of milk and two little mugs. And she said, " What's that for ? "

And Milly-Molly-Mandy said, " That's for our supper. But it isn't time to eat it yet. Mother says we can warm the milk on the stove, if we like, in a saucepan."

" What fun ! " said little-friend-Susan. " Then we'll be cooks. Couldn't we do something to the bread - and - dripping too ? "

So Milly-Molly-Mandy looked at the bread - and - dripping

thoughtfully, and then she said, " We could toast it— at the fire ! "

" Oh, yes ! " said little-friend-Susan. And then she said, " Oughtn't we to begin doing it now ? It takes quite a long time to cook things."

So Milly-Molly-Mandy said, " Let's ! " and fetched a saucepan, and little-friend-Susan took up the jug of milk, and then—suddenly—" Bang-bang-BANG ! " went the door-knocker, ever so loudly.

" Ooh ! " said little-friend-Susan, " that did make me jump ! I wonder who it is ! "

" Ooh ! " said Milly-Molly-Mandy. " We mustn't open the door unless we know. I wonder who it can be ! "

So together they went to the door, and Milly-Molly-Mandy put her mouth to the letter-box and said politely, " Please, who are you, please ? "

Milly-Molly-Mandy

Nobody spoke for a moment; and then a funny sort of voice outside said very gruffly, "I'm Mr Snooks."

And directly they heard that Milly-Molly-Mandy and little-friend-Susan looked at each other and said both together—"It's Billy Blunt!" And they unlocked the door and pulled it open.

And there was Billy Blunt standing grinning on the doorstep!

Milly-Molly-Mandy held the door wide for him to come in, and she said, "Did you think we didn't know you?"

And little-friend-Susan said, "You did give us a jump!" And Billy Blunt came in, grinning all over his face.

"We're all alone," said Milly-Molly-Mandy. "We're keeping house."

"Look at our aprons," said little-friend-Susan. "We're going to cook our suppers."

"Come on," said Milly-Molly-Mandy, "and we'll give you some. May you stop?"

Billy Blunt let them pull him into the kitchen, and then he said he'd seen Father and Mother and Grandpa and Grandma and Uncle and Aunty as they went past the corn-shop to the cross-roads, and Mother had told him they were alone, and that he could go and have a game with them if he liked. So he thought he'd come and give them a jump.

"Take your coat off, because it's hot in here," said

Keeps House

Milly-Molly-Mandy. " Now we must get on with the cooking. Come on, Susan ! "

So they put the milk into the saucepan on the back of the stove, and then they each took a piece of bread-and-dripping on a fork, to toast it.

But it wasn't a very good ' toasting fire ' (or else there were too many people trying to toast at the same time). Billy Blunt began to think it was rather long to wait, and he looked at the frying-pan on the side of the stove (in which Mother always cooked the breakfast bacon), and said, " Why not put 'em in there and fry 'em up ? "

Milly-Molly-Mandy and little-friend-Susan thought that was a splendid idea ; so they fried all the bread-and-dripping nice and brown (and it did smell good !). When they had done it there was just a little fat left in the pan, so they looked round for something else to cook.

" I'll go and see if there're any odd bits of bread in the bread-crock," said Milly-Molly-Mandy. " We mustn't cut any, because I'm not allowed to use the bread-knife yet."

So she went into the scullery to look, and there were one or two dry pieces in the bread-crock. But she found something else, and that was—a big basket of onions ! Then Milly-Molly-Mandy gave a little squeal, because she had a good idea, and she took out a small onion (she knew she might, because they had lots, and Father grew them) and ran back into the kitchen with it.

And Billy Blunt, with his scout's-knife, peeled it and sliced it into the pan (and the onion made him cry like anything !) ; and then Milly-Molly-Mandy fried it on

the stove (and the onion made *her* cry like anything !) ;
and then little-friend-Susan, who didn't want to be out
of any fun, stirred it up, with her head well over the pan
(and the onion made her cry like anything too !—at
least, she managed to get one small tear out).

And the onion smelt most delicious, all over the
kitchen—only it would seem to cook all black or else
not at all. But you can't *think* how
good it tasted, spread on slices of fried
bread !

They all sat on the hearthrug before
the fire, with plates on their laps and
mugs by their sides, and divided everything as evenly as possible. And they
only wished there was more of everything
(for of course Mother hadn't thought of
Billy Blunt when she cut the bread-and-
dripping).

When they had just finished the last crumb the door
opened and Father and Mother and Grandpa and
Grandma and Uncle and Aunty came in. And they
all said together, " Whatever's all this smell of fried
onions ? "

So Milly-Molly-Mandy explained, and when Mother
had looked at the frying-pan to see that it wasn't burnt
(and it wasn't), she only laughed and opened the
window.

And Father said, " Well, this smell makes me feel
very hungry. Can't we have some fried onions for
supper too, Mother ? "

Then, before Father took little-friend-Susan and

And the onion smelt most delicious!

Billy Blunt home, Mother gave them all a piece of currant cake with which to finish their supper; and then she started frying a panful of onions for the grown-up supper.

And Milly-Molly-Mandy (when she had said good-bye to little-friend-Susan and Billy Blunt) watched Mother very carefully, so that she should know how to fry quite properly next time she was left to keep house!

XII

Milly-Molly-Mandy Goes Carol-singing

ONCE upon a time Milly-Molly-Mandy heard some funny sounds coming from the little garden at the side of Mr Blunt's corn-shop.

So she looked over the palings, and what should she see but Billy Blunt, looking very solemn and satisfied, blowing away on a big new shiny mouth-organ!

Milly-Molly-Mandy said, " Hullo, Billy ! " And Billy Blunt blew "Hullo!" into his mouth-organ (at least, Milly-Molly-Mandy guessed it was that), and went on playing.

Milly-Molly-Mandy waited a bit and listened, and suddenly she found she knew what he was playing. "It's *Good King Wenceslas* ! " said Milly-Molly-Mandy, "isn't it ? Can I have a go soon ? "

" I'm practising," said Billy Blunt, stopping for a moment and then going on again.

" Practising what ? " said Milly-Molly-Mandy.

Goes Carol-singing

" Carols," said Billy Blunt.

" What for ? " said Milly-Molly-Mandy.

" Don't know," said Billy Blunt, "only it's Christmas-time."

" Then we could go caroling ! " said Milly-Molly-Mandy, with a sudden thought. " You could play on your mouth-organ, and I could sing. We could do it outside people's houses on Christmas Eve. Ooh, let's ! "

But Billy Blunt only said " Huh ! " and went on blowing his mouth-organ. But he did it rather thoughtfully.

Milly-Molly-Mandy waited a bit longer, and then she was just going to say good-bye when Billy Blunt said, " Here ! You can have a go if you want to."

So Milly-Molly-Mandy, very pleased, took the mouth-organ and wiped it on her skirt, and had quite a good 'go' (and Billy Blunt knew she was playing *God Save the King*). And then she wiped it again and gave it back, saying, " Good-bye, Billy. Don't forget about the carol-singing," and went on homeward up the white road with the hedges each side.

A few days later (it was the day before Christmas Eve) Billy Blunt came up to the nice white cottage with the thatched roof, where Milly-Molly-Mandy lived, to bring a bag of meal which Uncle had ordered from

Milly-Molly-Mandy

Mr Blunt's corn-shop for his chickens. Milly-Molly-Mandy was watching Father cut branches of holly from the holly-tree; but when she saw Billy Blunt she thought of the carols, and came running down to the path.

"I say," said Billy Blunt. "About that carol-singing."

"Yes!" said Milly-Molly-Mandy. "Have you been practising hard?"

"Mmm," said Billy Blunt, "I thought we might try 'em over now, if you're still keen on it. Where'll we do it?"

So Milly-Molly-Mandy led the way to the barn; and there in private they made plans and tried over one or two songs. They couldn't do *Hark the Herald Angels Sing* or *Christians Awake*, as the top notes in both of them went beyond the top of the mouth-organ, and Billy Blunt wouldn't sing the top notes, because he said it didn't sound proper. But he could play *Noël* and *While Shepherds Watched* and *Wenceslas* beautifully. So Milly-Molly-Mandy sang while Billy Blunt played, until they could do it together quite nicely.

"I'll have to ask Mother first if I may," said Milly-Molly-Mandy then. So they went round the back way into the kitchen, where Mother and Grandma and Aunty were mixing the Christmas pudding, and Milly-Molly-Mandy asked her question.

Goes Carol-singing

Just at first Mother looked a little doubtful. And then she said, " You know Christmas-time is giving time. If you don't mean to knock at the doors and sing for money——"

Milly-Molly-Mandy said, " No, we won't."

" Why, that would be very nice, then," said Mother, ' if you do it as nicely as ever you can."

" We'll do it our very best, just for love," said Milly-Molly-Mandy ; and Billy Blunt nodded. Then Mother gave them some almonds and bits of peel-sugar, and then Billy Blunt had to go back.

The next day, directly tea was over, Milly-Molly-Mandy, very excited, slipped out of the house in her hat and coat and muffler, and ran down to the gate to look for Billy Blunt.

It was very dark. Presently she saw a bicycle lamp coming along the road. It was jogging up and down in a queer way for a bicycle. And then as it came near it started waving to and fro, and Milly-Molly-Mandy guessed there must be Billy Blunt with it ; and she skipped up and down outside the gate, because it did look so exciting and Christmassy !

" You ready ? Come on," said Billy Blunt, and the two of them set off down the road.

Milly-Molly-Mandy

Soon they came to the Moggs's cottage, and began their carols. At the end of the first song little-friend-Susan's head peered from behind the window curtain ; and in the middle of the second she came rushing out of the door, saying, " Oh, wait a bit while I get my hat and coat on, and let me join ! "

And Mrs Moggs called from inside, " Susan, bring them in quickly and shut that door, you're chilling the house ! "

So they hurried inside and shut the door ; and there was Mrs Moggs sitting by the fire with Baby Moggs in her lap, and Mr Moggs was fixing a bunch of holly over the mantelpiece. Mrs Moggs gave them each a lump of toffee, and then Milly-Molly-Mandy and Billy Blunt with little-friend-Susan went off to their caroling.

When they came to the village they meant to sing outside Mr Blunt's corn-shop, and Miss Muggins's draper's shop; but all the little shop-windows were so brightly lit up it made them feel shy.

People were going in and out of Mr Smale the Grocer's shop, and Mrs Hubble the Baker's shop, and sometimes they stopped to look in Miss Muggins's window (which was showing a lot of gay little penny toys and strings of tinsel balls, as well as gloves and handkerchiefs).

Milly-Molly-Mandy said, " Let's wait ! " and Billy Blunt said, " Come on ! " So they turned into the dark lane by the forge.

They heard the *cling-clang* of a hammer banging on the anvil. And Milly-Molly-Mandy said, " Let's sing to Mr Rudge ! " So they went up to the half-open door of the forge.

They started on their carol

Milly-Molly-Mandy

Billy Blunt blew a little note on the mouth-organ, and they started on their carol.

By the end of the first verse the Blacksmith was bringing his hammer down in time to the music, and it sounded just like a big bell chiming ; and then he began

joining in, in a big humming sort of voice. And when they finished he shouted out, "Come on in and give us some more!"

So Milly-Molly-Mandy and Billy Blunt and little-friend-Susan came in out of the dark.

It was lovely in the forge, so warm, and full of strange shadows and burnt-leathery sort of smells. They had a warm-up by the fire, and then began another song. And the Blacksmith sang and hammered all to time ; and it sounded—as Mr Jakes the Postman popped his head in to say—"real nice and Christmassy!"

"Go on, give us some more," said the Blacksmith, burying his horseshoe in the fire again to make it hot, so that he could punch nail-holes in it.

"We can't do many more," said Milly-Molly-Mandy, "because the mouth-organ isn't quite big enough."

"Oh, never mind that," said the Blacksmith. "Go on, William, give us *Hark the Herald Angels Sing!*"

Goes Carol-singing

So Billy Blunt grinned and struck up, and everybody joined in so lustily that nobody noticed the missing top notes. While they were in the middle of it the door creaked open a little wider, and Miss Muggins's Jilly slipped in to join the fun; and later on Mr and Mrs Blunt strolled over (when they had shut up shop); and then Mr Critch the Thatcher. And soon it seemed as if half the village were in and round the old forge, singing away, song after song, while the Blacksmith hammered like big bells on his anvil, and got all his horseshoes finished in good time before the holidays.

Presently who should come in but Father! He had been standing outside for quite a time, listening with Mother and Uncle and Aunty and Mr Moggs (they had all strolled down to see what their children were up to, and stopped to join the singing).

But soon Mother beckoned to Milly-Molly-Mandy from behind Father's shoulder, and Miss Muggins peeped round the door and beckoned to Jilly, and Mrs Blunt beckoned to Billy Blunt, and Mr Moggs to little-friend-Susan. They knew that meant bed, but for once they didn't much mind, because it would make Christmas come all the sooner!

So the carols came to an end, and the Blacksmith called out, "What about passing the hat for the carolers?"

But Billy Blunt said with a grin, "You sang, too—louder than we did!"

And little-friend-Susan said, "Everybody sang!"

And Milly-Molly-Mandy said, "We did it for love—all of us!"

Milly-Molly-Mandy

And everybody said, " So we did, now ! " and wished everybody else " Happy Christmas ! "

And then Milly-Molly-Mandy said, " Good night, see you to-morrow ! " to Billy Blunt, and went skipping off home to bed, holding on to Father's hand through the dark.

" PEACE ON EARTH · GOODWILL TO MEN "